SUGAR IN MILK

by **Thrity Umrigar**
Illustrated by **Khoa Le**

RP|KIDS
PHILADELPHIA

Running Press Kids
Hachette Book Group
1290 Avenue of the Americas, New York, NY 10104
www.runningpress.com/rpkids
@RP_Kids

Printed in China

First Edition: October 2020

Published by Running Press Kids, an imprint of Perseus Books, LLC,
a subsidiary of Hachette Book Group, Inc. The Running Press Kids name and
logo is a trademark of the Hachette Book Group.

The Hachette Speakers Bureau provides a wide range of authors
for speaking events. To find out more, go to www.hachettespeakersbureau.com
or call (866) 376-6591.

The publisher is not responsible for websites (or their content)
that are not owned by the publisher.

Print book cover and interior design by Frances J. Soo Ping Chow

Library of Congress Control Number: 2019934248

ISBNs: 978-0-7624-9519-1 (hardcover), 978-0-7624-9521-4 (ebook),
978-0-7624-9544-3 (ebook), 978-0-7624-9545-0 (ebook)

APS

10 9 8 7 6 5 4

For my beloved dad, Noshir Umrigar,
who taught me the ancient lesson of good thoughts,
good words, good deeds.

—T. U.

When I first came to this country,
I felt so alone.

I knew Auntie and Uncle were happy to have me.

They filled my room
with books and toys
and painted it purple—
my favorite color.

But my friends and my family
were all back home.

I missed my mom and dad
and my cats, Kulfi and Baklava, too.

After Auntie and Uncle left for work,
I sat alone in my room,

thinking of my old friends and
longing to make new ones.

Uncle and Auntie were worried
but didn't know how to help me.

Then, one day, Auntie came into my room.
"Let's go for a walk," she said with a smile.
As we walked, Auntie told me a story:

There
once lived a group of people
in the ancient land of Persia
who were forced to leave their home
and seek refuge elsewhere.

"Come, my people," said their leader.
"Now that we have to leave
the home we love so much,
we must find a new land that we can
call our own."

So they built a few boats
and sailed the mighty sea
until they arrived at the shores of India
and begged to be given shelter.

But the local king did not want
to let them in.
"Our land is too crowded," he grumbled,
"with no room for others.
Besides, these visitors look foreign
and speak a strange and different language
I do not understand."

The king went to the seashore
where the ragged travelers stood
and ordered them to leave.
But, they couldn't understand him
(because he spoke a strange and
different language
they did not understand).

The king sighed impatiently.
He snapped his fingers
and ordered his servant to bring him
an empty glass.

He filled the glass with milk
all the way to the very top
and silently pointed to it.

It was his way of saying:
"My apologies to you.
I would've loved to help.
You look like very fine people
(even though you speak a strange
and different language
I do not understand).

But just as this glass is filled to the brim
with no room for more,
so are we full up
in my little, crowded kingdom."

The travelers had come from afar,
and they were tired and hungry and cold.
And very sad to be turned away.

Just then their leader spoke.
He was a small and clever man
with an ever-present smile on his lips.

"Just a minute, O Mighty King," he said.
"A moment, sir, of your time."

And before the king could speak,
the leader dug into his old, tattered sack
and pulled out a spoonful of sugar.

He stirred the sugar into the glass
slowly,
carefully,
dissolving every grain of sugar,
making sure he didn't spill
a single drop of milk.

He smiled as he pointed silently
to the king's glass.

Between two wise people,
sometimes words are not necessary.

The king understood what the leader meant:
If you let us stay, O Mighty King,
we will live in peace beside all of you.

And just like sugar in milk,
we will sweeten your lives
with our presence.

The king stared at the sweetened milk.
His lips twitched.
First, he smiled.
Then, he grinned.
And finally,
he roared with laughter.

The king hugged the group of travelers.
"Welcome to your new home,"
he cried.
"May you live with us forever,
in peace and joy."

And even though the strangers
didn't follow a word the king said
(because he spoke a strange
and different language
they did not understand),

everybody knows what a hug means.
And all people speak the language of laughter.
So, no one had a problem
understanding what the other meant.

Thus, the Persians stayed.
India became their new home.
And they kept their ancient promise
of spreading happiness wherever they went.

After Auntie finished
telling me this old story,
we walked quietly for a few moments.

I looked around me, stopped.
And then I took another step—
into the dazzling light of America.

Nothing had changed.
And yet, everything had.

I began to smile at the people we passed,
and they returned my smile.
Everybody I said hello to said hello back to me.
Even the dogs seemed friendlier
and wagged their tails faster.

I laughed out loud and wondered why
I had ever been sad or lonely
in such a welcoming place.

The next day, when I left the house,
I asked Auntie for a pack of sugar.
I kept it in my pocket
to remind me to make things sweeter
wherever I wandered . . .

in my new and magical homeland.